DISNEP · PIXAR

DISCARD

The Junior Novelization

Adapted by Leslie Goldman
Inspired by the art and character designs
created by Pixar

Random House 🏠 **New York**

DISCARD

Library of Congress Control Number: 2009926426

ISBN: 978-0-7364-2652-7

www.randomhouse.com/kids

Printed in the United States of America

10 9 8 7 6 5 4 3 2 1

Chapter

Buzz Lightyear sped through the dark sky, his jet engines shooting out sparks as he blasted over the surface of a huge planet. He navigated around rocks and craters, then landed smoothly. He glanced up and down the surface of the deserted planet before raising his wrist communicator. "Buzz Lightyear Mission Log: all signs point to this planet as the location of Zurg's fortress. But there seems to be no sign of intelligent life anywhere."

Just then, a cluster of red laser beams landed on Buzz. He looked up to discover that he was surrounded by armed robot forces—and they were all aiming their weapons right at him! Buzz dove across the ground and fired his laser at a group of rock crystals. The crystals reflected his laser beam back at the crowd of robots, creating a huge explosion. The force of the explosion blasted the robots away and threw Buzz into a crater, robot parts raining down around him. He ran to the wall of the crater for cover, and a robotic camera popped out of it. The camera trained its sights right on Buzz. Quickly, he took aim once more and fired.

The camera was destroyed, but then the ground began to shift under his feet. Suddenly, a hole opened up beneath Buzz, and he jumped into a deep, dark cavern before the hole closed above him once again. He landed on the ground and turned on his space suit's glow-in-the-dark feature before running into what looked like a tunnel.

As he made his way through the tunnel, Buzz didn't realize that the evil Emperor Zurg was monitoring his every step from a control room. Zurg let out an evil laugh. "Come to me, my prey," he growled.

Suddenly, the lights in the tunnel came on. Buzz stopped and turned around just as a door slammed shut behind him. Deadly spikes shot out of the door and began to zoom toward Buzz. He turned and ran as fast as he could through the tunnel, the spikes following behind. As Buzz ran, he saw another door up ahead—but it was starting to close! He took a giant leap and made it through the door without a millisecond to spare. *Crash!* The spikes banged against the closed door, denting the exterior behind him.

Buzz stood at the edge of a chasm. On the other side, the source of Zurg's power hung suspended in a force field. It was a small object that looked like a battery. Buzz had to reach it, so he stepped onto a bridge made up of disks that were suspended in the air. He jumped carefully from disk to disk, each one letting out an ominous musical note as he made his way across. Without warning, the disks suddenly fell away, sending Buzz into a free fall.

Buzz pushed a button on his utility belt,

creating a clear bubble that encased him and allowed him to zoom back up to the ledge where Zurg's power source was located. When he landed safely, the bubble burst, and Buzz reached for the power source—but it disappeared. It had been an illusion!

Suddenly, Buzz heard Zurg's sinister voice. He turned to find the evil robot rising up behind him. "So we meet again, Buzz Lightyear . . . for the last time," sneered Zurg.

"Not today, Zurg!" shouted Buzz.

Zurg took aim with his ion blaster and began to fire at Buzz, but Buzz managed to grab one of the disks that had been part of the bridge and use it as a shield. Zurg's shots bounced right off it. Buzz then hurled the shield at Zurg, hitting him directly in the face.

"Ohh . . . ," moaned a stunned Zurg.

Taking advantage of Zurg's momentary weakness, Buzz leaped over him and fired one shot. It careened to Zurg's left, narrowly missing its target.

Zurg recovered and took aim again. This time he hit Buzz. "Ah-ha-ha!" Zurg laughed triumphantly.

Suddenly, the words GAME OVER flashed in red across a television screen.

"No, no, no, no, no!" Rex, a plastic T. rex, shouted. He was holding a video game controller. Next to him, Buzz Lightyear, the space ranger toy, smiled encouragingly. "Oh, you almost had him!" said Buzz.

Sun streamed in through the windows of Andy Davis's bedroom, where his toys stood atop his desk, battling the evil Zurg in a video game. Since Andy was not in the room, his toys were moving around on their own, just as they always did when people weren't watching. Rex loved playing the Buzz Lightyear video game, and he had been determined to beat the evil Zurg, but now he was slumped in failure.

"I'm never gonna defeat Zurg!" he cried.

"Sure you will, Rex. In fact, you're a better Buzz than I am," replied Buzz.

"But look at my little arms. I can't press the Fire button and jump at the same time!" moaned Rex as he motioned to the buttons that controlled both movements.

Suddenly, the toys heard a loud crash coming from Andy's dresser. They looked up to see Woody the cowboy toy rummaging impatiently through one of the drawers, tossing junk to the floor. "Where is it?" he asked himself over and over.

"Uh, Woody?" asked Buzz with concern.

Startled by Buzz's voice, Woody stood up and smacked his head on the open drawer directly above him. The impact sent him tumbling out of the drawer he was in. He hit another drawer before landing hard on the floor below.

"Hang on, cowboy!" shouted Buzz. He launched himself down to the floor and landed expertly in front of Woody.

"Woody, are you all right?" asked Buzz.

"Oh, yeah, I'm fine, Buzz." But Woody didn't look fine. He looked frazzled as he continued talking nervously. "Okay, here's a list of things to do while I'm gone. Batteries need to be changed. Toys in the bottom of the chest need to be rotated. Oh, and make sure everyone attends Mr. Spell's seminar on what to do if you or a part of you is swallowed. Okay? Okay. Good."

Buzz shook his head calmly. "Woody, you haven't found your hat yet, have you?"

"No!" exclaimed Woody, suddenly showing complete panic. "Andy's leaving for Cowboy Camp any minute, and I can't find it anywhere!"

"Don't worry. In just a few hours you'll be sitting around a campfire with Andy making delicious hot schmoes," said Buzz.

"They're called s'mores, Buzz," Woody corrected him.

"Right," said Buzz, nodding. "Has anyone found Woody's hat yet?" he called to the rest of the toys.

The Green Army Men swarmed around the open toy box. Some slid down ropes from the lid into the box. "Hut! Hut! Hut!" they chanted.

From the edge of the toy box, Sarge saluted Buzz and Woody. "Negatory. Still searching."

Hamm, a plastic piggy bank, sat on the window sill and pulled the blinds open and shut, as if signaling someone outside. Lenny, a pair of toy binoculars, peered through the window. "The lawn gnome next door says it's not in the yard, but he'll keep looking," Hamm reported.

A porcelain Bo Peep figurine walked into the room. "It's not in Molly's room. We've looked everywhere," she said. Molly was Andy's little sister, and everyone knew that Andy's toys sometimes ended up with her.

Woody walked over to Andy's backpack, which was lying on the floor. He peered inside. No hat. "Great. That's just great! This'll be the first year I miss Cowboy Camp, all because of my stupid hat."

"Woody, look under your boot," said Bo Peep.

"Bo, don't be silly. My hat's not under my boot," replied Woody.

"Just look," she said.

Woody sighed and then raised his foot and looked at it. The word ANDY had been written on the sole with a marker. "You see? No hat. Just the word *Andy*."

"Uh-huh," said Bo, smiling. "And the boy who wrote that would take you to camp with or without your hat."

Woody smiled apologetically as he stared at the signature. Bo was right. "I'm sorry, Bo. It's just that I've been looking forward to this all year. It's my one time with just me and Andy."

Bo grinned, then snared Woody with her shepherd's crook. She pulled him toward her. "You're cute when you care," she cooed.

"Bo, not in front of Buzz," whispered a blushing Woody.

"Let him look," she said, leaning forward to kiss Woody.

Suddenly, Bo's sheep began to baa. Woody and Bo looked up to find Rex and the sheep in a tug-of-war over the cord of the video game controller.

"Uh, Miss Peep? Your sheep!" exclaimed an

overwhelmed Rex. Bo Peep gave a loud whistle, and the sheep immediately let go of the cord. Rex fell backward and landed on the remote control. The TV turned on, blasting a commercial for Al's Toy Barn, the local toy store.

"Hey, kids, this is Al, from Al's Toy Barn!" came a voice from the TV. The toys watched as a large man in a chicken suit flapped his fake wings and hopped around in front of Al's Toy Barn. "I'm sitting on some good deals here. I think I'm feeling a deal hatching right now! Let's see what we got!" A bell pinged, and the camera focused on the ground near the man's feet, revealing a cartoon egg. It cracked open, and pictures of toys began to float across the screen. "We got boats for a buck, beanies for a buck, boomerangs . . . ," Al continued.

"Turn it off!" shouted Woody. "Someone's going to hear!" Rex ran to the remote and stomped on it over and over. But he couldn't figure out which button would turn the TV off.

The TV continued to blare as Al flapped his

chicken wings. "And that's cheap, cheap, cheap!" A map flashed on the screen, and Al pointed to the Toy Barn. "So hurry on down!"

Hamm waddled forward and grabbed the remote. "For crying out loud, it's this one!" He pushed the Power button and the TV shut off. "I despise that chicken."

"Ahh!" Woody exclaimed in relief.

Suddenly, Slinky Dog came through the door. Or at least the front of his body did—the coils of his wiry body remained in the hallway. "Fellas!" he called. "Okay, I got some good news and I got some bad news."

"What? What is it?" asked the toys. They all looked at Slinky anxiously.

"Good news is, I found your hat, Woody." Slinky's back end padded into the room, tail wagging. Woody's hat was perched right on top of it.

"My hat!" shouted Woody. "Aw, Slink. Thank you! Thank you, thank you, thank you, thank you! Where did you find it?"

"Well, that's the bad news," replied Slinky.

Suddenly, a dog's bark sounded from the hall. The bark grew louder and more excited as the dog approached.

"Aaah! It's Buster!" shouted Rex.

The Green Army Men and Rocky Gibraltar, the toy strongman, rushed to the door and closed it quickly in an attempt to keep out Andy's over-eager puppy. But they were too slow, and the door didn't click shut. Rocky strained, but Buster was pushing too hard from the other side. The dog's wet nose nudged through the crack in the door. And the toys knew it wasn't stopping there.

Chapter

"**W**oody! Hide! Quick!" called Bo.

Woody looked around desperately and ran for cover. Then the door burst open, and Buster, a caramel-colored dachshund, rushed into the room. He barked loudly and ran in circles, scattering toys and drool everywhere.

Suddenly, Buster sniffed and turned toward Andy's backpack. He ran over to the bag and buried his nose in an open compartment. Growling, he dragged Woody out and flung the limp cowboy across the room. Woody landed in the center of the room, where Buster jumped on top of him. The little dog snarled for a second, then began to lick Woody excitedly.

"Okay, okay," sputtered Woody. "You found me,

Buster. All right. Hey, how did he do, Hamm?"

Hamm stood in front of Mr. Spell's readout: 13.5 seconds. "Looks like a new record!"

Woody snapped his fingers. "Okay, boy. Sit. Reach for the sky! Pow!"

With a happy yelp, Buster fell over and played dead.

"Great job, boy," said Woody, scratching Buster's belly. "Who's gonna miss me while I'm gone? Who's gonna miss me?" Buster kicked his legs with delight.

Suddenly, voices from the hallway drifted into Andy's bedroom.

"Andy? Have you got all your stuff?" asked Andy's mom, Mrs. Davis.

Woody gasped and ran off to take his position. "Okay, have a good weekend, everybody," he whispered hurriedly. "I'll see you Sunday night." All the other toys froze where they were and lay motionless.

"It's in my room," they heard Andy call from outside the door. Then Andy kicked his bedroom door open wide. Buster barked and ran toward the boy happily. "Stick 'em up!" shouted Andy, pointing his fingers toward the dog as if he were arresting an outlaw. Buster paused to scratch his ear, then ran between Andy's legs and out of the room.

"I guess we'll work on that later," Andy sighed. He walked over to Woody, who was propped up on his backpack. "Hey, Woody. Ready to go to Cowboy Camp?"

"Andy, honey," called his mother. "Five minutes and we're leaving."

"Five minutes . . . hmmm," said Andy, eyeing his toys.

In no time, the scene was set. "Somebody help me!" said Andy in a high-pitched voice, pretending to be Bo Peep as she hung in the air from a string. Then he grabbed Woody.

"Let her go, evil Dr. Pork Chop!" Andy said, pretending to be Woody.

"Never! You must choose, Sheriff Woody." Andy gave Hamm a menacing voice as the piggy bank stood over a formation of Green Army Men. "How shall she die? By shark, or death by monkeys? Choose!" Andy dangled Bo first over a rubber shark, then over plastic monkeys.

"I choose . . . Buzz Lightyear!" shouted Andy as Woody. Andy put RC Car's remote control in front of Woody and pressed a button. A whirring sound filled the air, and the toy car shot out of a cardboard box, with Buzz riding on top. The two went over a ramp and smashed into Hamm.

"To infinity . . . and beyond!" Andy cried triumphantly as Buzz. "You should never tangle with the unstoppable duo of Woody and Buzz Lightyear!"

Andy made Buzz and Woody link arms. Suddenly, Woody's arm ripped!

"Oh, no," said Andy sadly.

"Andy, let's go," called Mrs. Davis. She poked her head into Andy's room.

"But, Mom, Woody's arm ripped," replied Andy.

Mrs. Davis took Woody from Andy. "Maybe we can fix him on the way," she suggested.

"No, just leave him." Andy sighed.

"I'm sorry, honey. But you know toys don't last forever." Mrs. Davis placed Woody on the highest shelf in the room, amid a pile of old books. Then she and Andy left.

Once they were alone, the toys blinked and sat up. They stared up at Woody. "What happened?" asked Rex, shocked that Woody had been left behind.

Woody stared in disbelief at his ripped arm. Then he scrambled to the edge of his shelf and looked out the window. Andy and his mother were getting into their van.

"Andy!" he cried. He watched sadly as the van pulled away, then slumped to the back of the shelf.

The next morning, Woody was shaken from his sleep by the sound of a van pulling up in front of the house. Once more, he looked out the window. Andy jumped out of the van.

"He's back?" Woody whispered. He glanced down. Rex, Slinky, and Rocky were playing cards at the foot of the bed. "Hey, everybody! Andy's back! He's back early from Cowboy Camp!" The toys didn't respond. Then they heard Andy bounding up the steps.

"Places, everybody! Andy's coming!" yelled Hamm.

The toys dropped their cards and scattered. Woody froze in his toy pose just as Andy burst into the room riding a hobbyhorse. "Yee-haw!" Andy cried.

Andy ran up to Woody and pulled him down from the shelf. "Hey, Woody! Did you miss me?"

"Giddyap, giddyap. Ride 'em, cowboy!" Andy ran around the room, swinging Woody along. Suddenly, Andy's smile faded as he caught sight of Woody's shoulder. "Oh, I forgot," he said to Woody. "You're broken." He stared at Woody, frowning. "I don't want to play with you any-more."

And with that, Andy dropped Woody.

Woody fell in slow motion, down into the pile of scattered cards—every one was an ace of spades. And then he fell even farther, through the cards, through the floor, down a long, dark passage. When he finally landed, he was at the bottom of a trash can. A single spotlight shone down on him, and he suddenly realized that he was lying atop a pile of broken doll parts. He jumped with fright and tried to crawl out of the can, but a swarm of toy arms pulled him back down again. "Andy!" he yelled, continuing to struggle.

Andy peered down into the can. "Bye, Woody," he called sadly, his voice echoing.

"No . . . Andy!" Woody cried. But it was too late. Andy closed the lid, and everything went black.

"Ahhhh!" Woody screamed, waking himself with a start. He was still on Andy's shelf. He glanced around the room in confusion—until he realized that it had all been a bad dream. Woody was relieved, but then he remembered his broken arm, which hung limp around his neck. Disgusted, he swung his arm off his neck, knocking over a pile of books. A cloud of dust rose, and Woody coughed. Soon he noticed that he wasn't the only one coughing. He began to search the shelf, following a series of coughs and wheezy squeaks. With his good arm, he pushed aside a book covered in cobwebs to find a lonely squeeze toy.

"Wheezy? Is that you?" he asked a sad-looking penguin.

"Hey, Woody," gasped Wheezy.

"What are you doing up here? I thought Mom took you to get your squeaker fixed months ago. Andy was so upset," said Woody, confused.

"Nah," said Wheezy, motioning with one dust-covered wing. "She just told him that to calm him down. Then she put me on the shelf."

"Why didn't you yell for help?" asked Woody.

"I tried squeaking," Wheezy said with a shrug.

"But I'm still broken. No one could hear me." He squinted and tried to squeak. The only sound that emerged was a pathetic little gasp. "The dust aggravates my condition." Wheezy had a coughing fit and then fell into Woody's arms, exhausted.

"What's the point of prolonging the inevitable?" Wheezy said, struggling to speak. "We're all just one stitch away from here . . . to there." He pointed outside. Woody looked out the window and gasped. Mrs. Davis was pounding a sign into the ground that read YARD SALE.

Woody's eyes widened. He called down to the other toys. "Yard sale! Guys! Wake up! There's a yard sale outside!"

Buzz and Slinky stirred from their snooze. "Yard sale?" repeated Buzz. More toys popped their heads out of Andy's toy chest.

"Sarge! Emergency roll call," said Woody.

Sarge burst out from the Bucket o' Soldiers and gave Woody a salute.

"Sir! Yes, sir!" He went around to gather all the

toys. "Red Alert!" he called. "All civilians fall into position! Now! Single file! Let's move, move, move!"

The toys responded quickly and lined up.

Buzz marched over and began to call out the name of each toy.

"Hamm?" he called.

"Here!" Hamm shouted. Buzz continued the roll call, making sure that all the toys were accounted for, until they heard footsteps outside Andy's door.

"Ahhh! Someone's coming!" Rex cried.

The toys ran back to their previous positions and froze. Woody hid Wheezy back behind the book on the shelf and then returned to his old place just as the door began to creak open.

Mrs. Davis entered the room with a box marked 25 CENTS. She reached under Andy's bed and dug out a pair of roller skates, then placed them in the box. She picked up Rex, who tried to hide his look of utter panic. She put him down again and picked up the game he had been sitting on. Next she reached up to the shelf where Woody and Wheezy were sitting. She took the book that was hiding Wheezy. Thinking she was done, Woody sighed with relief. But seconds later, Mrs. Davis reached up again . . . and grabbed Wheezy! "Bye, Woody," the penguin whispered as he was dropped into the box and carried out of the room.

Woody panicked. "Wheezy! Think, think, Woody, think." He had to do something. Woody raised his good arm to his mouth and let out a loud whistle. Buster came bounding into the room. "Here, boy. Here, Buster, up here!" called Woody.

He tried to climb down from the shelf but slipped and fell because of his bad arm. Buster ran toward Woody and was able to catch him before he crashed onto the hardwood floor.

Woody propped himself up on Buster's back and patted his fur. "Okay, boy, to the yard sale."

"What's going on?" the toys asked each other as Buster and Woody raced out of Andy's room.

"Don't do it, Woody! We love you!" cried Rex. The toys watched in disbelief, thinking Woody was about to put himself up for sale.

Chapter

At the front door, Woody and Buster paused before going out to the yard sale. They peered outside, checking to see if the coast was clear. "Okay, boy," Woody whispered into Buster's ear. "Let's go."

Woody held on to Buster's flank, trying to keep out of sight, as the little dog sauntered toward the table with the 25 CENTS box. Woody jumped onto the edge of the table. He hid for a moment behind a tall pepper grinder. Then he ran over to the box, hoisted himself up, and jumped inside.

Upstairs in Andy's room, the toys crowded around the window, trying to get a glimpse of Woody. They gasped when they saw him climb into the box.

"He's selling himself for twenty-five cents!" exclaimed Hamm.

"Oh, Woody, you're worth more than that," said Slinky sadly.

"Hold on, he's got something," said Buzz. "It's Wheezy!"

"It's a rescue!" exclaimed Rex, finally understanding.

Woody pushed Wheezy out of the box and then jumped to the ground himself. Woody tucked Wheezy under Buster's collar.

"There you go, pal," he said once he was sure the toy penguin was secure.

"Bless you, Woody," wheezed Wheezy.

"All right now, back to Andy's room," Woody said as he climbed onto Buster's back.

"Way to go, cowboy!" yelled the other toys, still watching from the window.

Buster bounded to victory, but Wheezy started to slip out from under the dog's collar.

"Woody, I'm slipping!" Wheezy cried.

With his good arm, Woody reached up and

secured Wheezy once again. Right then, Buster jumped over a toy in their path. Unable to hold on with only one arm, Woody was thrown to the ground. The oblivious Buster kept on running, leaving Woody flat on his back on the front walk.

Woody looked up to see Buster and Wheezy make their way into the house. Suddenly, a shadow passed over him. Woody went limp.

"Mommy, Mommy! Look at this!" yelled a little girl. "It's a cowboy dolly."

Back in Andy's room, the toys watched the scene in horror. "No, no, no," pleaded Buzz.

"That's not her toy!" shouted Rex.

"What's that little gal think she's doing?" asked Slinky.

The girl picked up Woody and ran to her mother. "Mommy, can we keep him? Please?"

"Oh, honey, you don't want that toy. It's broken," her mother said, staring at Woody's limp arm. She took Woody from her daughter and tossed him onto a nearby table just as the little girl tugged on Woody's pull string.

"There's a snake in my boot," came the voice from Woody's voice box as the pull string retracted.

When a heavy man standing nearby heard the voice, he gasped and ran over to Woody. He picked up the cowboy and began to examine him. "Original hand-painted face," he said excitedly. "Natural dyed blanket-stitched vest." Then he looked at Woody's torn arm. "Hmmm, a little rip . . . fixable. Oh, if only you had your hand-stitched polyvinyl—" The man suddenly spotted Woody's hat on the table. "Hat!" he yelped. "Oh, I found him! I found him! I found him!"

Mrs. Davis walked over to the man. "Excuse me. Can I help you?" she asked.

The man looked up nervously, gathering a few other items along with Woody. "Oh, ah, I'll give you, ah, fifty cents for all this junk."

"Oh, now, how did this get here?" said Mrs. Davis, reaching for Woody.

The man laughed. "Very well . . . five dollars."

"I'm sorry." Mrs. Davis shook her head. "It's an

old family toy." She took Woody from the man and began to walk away. But the man wouldn't give up. He got out his wallet and followed Mrs. Davis.

"Wait! I'll give you fifty bucks for him!" he said, waving the cash in front of Mrs. Davis.

"He's *not* for sale," she answered.

"Everything's for sale," reasoned the man. "Or trade. Ummm, you like my watch?"

"Sorry," said Mrs. Davis, shaking her head. She put Woody in the cashbox and locked it.

Though discouraged, the man was not ready to give up. He lurked around the yard sale, waiting for the perfect moment. When Mrs. Davis turned her back, he pried open the cashbox and grabbed Woody. He stuffed Woody into his bag and ran to his car.

Upstairs, the toys had been watching from Andy's window. They were horrified.

"Oh, no—he's stealing Woody!" exclaimed Buzz.

"Somebody do something!" cried Rex.

Without a moment's hesitation, Buzz leaped out the window and slid down a drainpipe. The toys watched helplessly as Buzz raced through the yard sale, hiding behind various objects on his way to the man's car.

Buzz made it to the street just as the man was pulling away from the house, tires screeching. Buzz ran as fast as he could after the car. He jumped for the bumper and was able to grab hold. He began trying to pry open the trunk, but the car hit a bump and he was thrown to the pavement.

Out of breath, Buzz managed to catch a glimpse of the car's license plate before it disappeared. It read LZTYBRN. That, along with several feathers that floated out of the car as it drove away, were his only clues as to who had taken Woody.

Inside the man's bag, Woody bounced around in the dark. Shaken and terrified, he wondered where he was going—and how he was going to get back to Andy. Suddenly, the car screeched to a stop. Woody heard the door open, and then he felt the bag being lifted out of the trunk. The bouncing began again, along with the steady beat of footsteps. Carefully, Woody peeked out of the bag. He looked up and saw the bearded face of the man who had stolen him. As the man carried Woody into an apartment building, Woody noticed a sign on the door and shuddered.

The sign read NO CHILDREN ALLOWED.

Back in Andy's room, the toys tried to come up with a plan to rescue Woody. Hamm paced in front of Etch A Sketch.

"All right," he said. "Let's review this one more time. At precisely eight-thirty-two-ish, Exhibit A, Woody, was kidnapped." He tapped his pointer on Etch, where Woody's figure was drawn. "Exhibit B: the composite sketch of the kidnapper."

Etch quickly erased Woody and then drew a fat

man with a beard that almost touched his feet.

"He didn't have a beard like that," protested Bo.

"Fine," said Hamm. "Etch, give him a shave."

Etch erased the man and drew another one, this time with a short beard.

"The kidnapper was bigger than that," said Slinky.

"Oh, picky, picky, picky," complained Hamm.

"How do you spell *FBI*?" asked Rex, holding a sign advertising a lost toy.

"Excuse me. A little quiet, please," said Buzz. He was studying Mr. Spell, whose screen was lit up with the letters LZTYBRN.

"Lazy-Toy-Brain," droned Mr. Spell's electronic voice as it attempted to make a word out of the mysterious letters. "Lousy-Try-Brian."

The toys approached Buzz. "What are you doing?" asked Rex.

"It's some sort of message encoded on that vehicle's ID tag," explained Buzz.

"Liz-Try-Bran," continued Mr. Spell.

None of the others believed that studying the license plate letters would help. "There are about three-point-five million registered cars in the tri-county area alone," said Hamm with resignation, turning back to Etch.

Buzz suddenly shouted, "Toy! Toy! Hold on!" He quickly punched more letters into Mr. Spell.

"Al's-Toy-Barn," said Mr. Spell.

"Al's Toy Barn?" cried the other toys. Everyone stopped in surprise.

Buzz picked up the feather he had found. A sudden realization came over him. He spun around and ran to Etch. "Etch, draw that man in a chicken suit!" he said.

When Etch finished the drawing, the toys stared in amazement. "It's the chicken man!" gasped Rex.

"That's our guy," said Buzz.

"I knew there was something I didn't like about that chicken," said Hamm.

Chapter

In his apartment, Al was stomping around in a chicken suit. He grabbed his cell phone and started yelling into it. "Yeah, yeah, yeah. I'll be right there. And we're gonna do this commercial in one take, do you hear me? Because I am in the middle of something really important!" He hung up and stared at Woody, who was now trapped inside a rectangular glass case.

"You, my little cowboy friend, are going to make me big"—he began to flap his wings—"buck-buck-bucks!" Al laughed and flapped his way out the apartment door.

When Al was gone, Woody rammed his shoulder into the door of the case. After a few pushes, he was able to open it. He jumped to the floor and rushed over to the door. The doorknob was way out of reach, and he couldn't open it. Instead, he jumped up to a chair and onto the windowsill, where he peered outside.

Woody gasped. There were tall buildings everywhere, and the street was far below. It was clear that Woody was a long way from home. "Andy," he said with a sigh.

He jumped down from the windowsill and began to explore Al's apartment. As he struggled with a heating grate, he heard a noise across the room. He turned around to see an open box filled with packing peanuts. From the box, a trail of peanuts led right to his feet. Woody was confused.

Suddenly, a floppy toy horse slipped between Woody's legs. "Whoa-oa-oa!" Woody yelled as the horse lifted him onto its back and began to leap around like a bucking bronco. Woody struggled to hang on. "Hey, stop! Horsey, stop! Sit, boy! Whoa!"

The horse stopped suddenly, causing Woody to

tumble forward to the floor. He landed on his head, looking backward and upside down through his splayed legs. That was when he noticed a cowgirl doll standing right in front of him. She stared back at Woody, bending down to his level with an eager grin on her face.

"Yeeeee-hawwww!" she yelled suddenly, grabbing Woody in a giant hug. "It's you! It's you!" She gave him a big noogie. "It's really *you*!"

"What's me?" asked Woody, startled.

"Whoo-ee!" cried the cowgirl, spinning Woody around. Holding on to his pull string, she yanked him back and caught him with her other arm. Then she put her ear to his chest and listened.

"There's a snake in my boot!" said Woody's voice box.

"Ha!" said the cowgirl, slapping Woody on the back. "It *is* you!"

"Please stop saying that," pleaded Woody. He had no idea what was going on.

"Prospector said someday you'd come!" the

cowgirl exclaimed. Then a look of realization flashed across her face. "The Prospector! He'll want to meet you!" She whistled to the horse, who dove into the cardboard box, dug around, and pulled out a smaller box. "Say hello to the Prospector!" the cowgirl announced excitedly.

"It's a box," said Woody, growing more confused by the minute.

"He's *mint* in the box," said the cowgirl. "Never been opened." The horse spun the box around to reveal an old miner doll with a white beard, tucked snugly in his unopened box.

"Oh, we've waited countless years for this day! It's so good to see you, Woody," said the Prospector. He was dressed in mining clothes, with a plastic pick hanging behind him in the box.

"Hey! How do you know my name?" asked Woody.

"Everyone knows *your* name, Woody," said the cowgirl.

"Why, you don't know who you are, do you?"

asked the Prospector. Then he turned to the others. "Bullseye?" he called, as if he were asking the little horse to do him a favor.

Bullseye galloped over to a pile of boxes, climbed up to a light switch, and turned on the lights with his nose. Woody glanced around the newly lit room and gasped. He was surrounded by a huge set of toys and all kinds of memorabilia, each one labeled WOODY'S ROUNDUP. And his picture was on every item.

There were a Woody yo-yo, a cereal box, plates, a radio, and even a magazine cover with a close-up of Woody's face.

"That's me," Woody said, amazed. He began to back up, bumping into a wall. When he turned and looked up, he realized it wasn't a wall at all—it was a giant cardboard cutout of himself. "Wow."

The Prospector nodded at Bullseye, and the horse pushed an old videotape into the player. The cowgirl, whose name was Jessie, turned on the TV with the remote, and a pair of barn doors flashed on the screen. A title card read COWBOY CRUNCHIES PRESENTS, and then an announcer's voice boomed, "Cowboy Crunchies, the only cereal that's sugar-frosted and dipped in chocolate, proudly presents . . . *Woody's Roundup!*"

The *Woody's Roundup* theme song began to play, and a black-and-white TV version of Jessie danced onto the screen. "Yo-de-lay-he-hoo!" she bellowed. A crowd of animals—skunks, rabbits, armadillos, a squirrel—came from every direction and surrounded Jessie.

"That's me!" cried Jessie. She jumped up and down and pointed at the screen enthusiastically. Woody stared from the screen to Jessie in awe.

The theme song continued, and Bullseye appeared. As the TV version of the horse played horseshoes on screen, the real Bullseye lowered his head modestly.

Next, the Prospector emerged from a cardboard mine on the screen. "Has anyone seen my pick?" he asked. He turned around to reveal his pick attached to his rear end, and a chorus of laughter rang out from an unseen TV audience.

The theme song came to an end, and Woody watched in disbelief as his on-screen self burst forward and leaped onto Bullseye, who reared up dramatically. An audience full of kids cheered as Woody waved his hat.

As the facts came together for Woody, his shock turned to joy. He began to understand that he had once been a big TV star!

Back at Andy's house, the toys gathered around the TV. They switched from channel to channel, searching for the Al's Toy Barn commercial.

"I can't find it!" cried Rex.

"Keep looking," said Buzz.

"Oh, you're going too slow," said Hamm in frustration. "Let me take the wheel." He bumped Rex aside and began flipping through the channels.

"It's too fast!" complained Rex.

Suddenly, the Al's Toy Barn commercial flashed past. The toys all began to shout.

"Stop! Back, back, back!" said Rex.

"Go back, Hamm!" yelled Slinky.

Hamm returned to the commercial just in time to hear Al exclaim, ". . . and look for the giant chicken!" A map flashed on the screen, and Buzz pointed to Etch.

"Now, Etch!" he ordered.

Etch quickly sketched a copy of the map right before the commercial ended. He placed a chicken on the spot that marked the Toy Barn.

"That's where I need to go," announced Buzz.

"You can't go, Buzz," said Rex. "You'll never make it there."

Buzz began to copy the map onto a piece of paper. "Woody once risked his life to save me. I couldn't call myself his friend if I weren't willing to do the same," he explained. "So who's with me?" He glanced around the room.

A short while later, as a group of brave toys prepared to leave, Bo Peep approached Buzz.

"This is for Woody—when you find him," she said. Then she gave Buzz a big kiss on the cheek.

Buzz blushed. "All right, but I don't think it'll mean the same coming from me."

As Bo walked away, Robot and Rocky carried Wheezy over to Buzz.

"Mr. Buzz Lightyear," Wheezy said weakly. "You've just got to save my pal Woody."

"I'll do my best," Buzz replied.

Then Buzz, Slinky, Rex, and Hamm climbed out the window and walked to the edge of the rooftop. Slinky acted as a bungee cord, allowing the toys to hold on to his rear legs as they jumped off the roof.

As Rex's turn approached, the toy dinosaur began to tremble with fear.

"You'd think with all my video game experience, I'd be feeling more prepared," he said nervously. Holding on to Slinky, he slipped and fell off the roof with a yell. A few seconds later, he appeared again, still holding on to Slinky and bouncing up and down with the dog's coil tail.

"The idea is to let go!" shouted Slinky.

Once Rex reached the ground safely, Buzz looked toward the window. "We'll be back before Andy gets home," he told the others. The toys inside gathered at the window and waved good-bye. "To Al's Toy Barn . . . and beyond!" yelled Buzz as he held on to Slinky and leaped off the roof. Slinky jumped last. The search for Woody had begun!

Chapter

Back in Al's apartment, Woody stared at the TV screen in awe. He, Jessie, Bullseye, and the Prospector had been watching old episodes of *Woody's Roundup* for hours.

"Next tape!" Woody shouted when an episode featuring a dramatic cliffhanger came to an end. Jessie stood up and clicked the TV off with her boot.

"Wait a minute!" exclaimed Woody. "What happened? Come on, let's see the next episode!"

"That's it," said the Prospector.

"What?" asked Woody.

"The show was canceled after that," the Prospector explained.

"What about the gold mine and the cute little

critters and the dynamite?" asked Woody. "It was a great show! Why cancel it?"

"Two words," replied the Prospector. "*Sput-nik.* Once the astronauts went up, children only wanted to play with space toys."

"I know how that feels," said Woody, thinking back to his early relationship with Buzz. He glanced at the Roundup collection surrounding him. "But still, my own show. Look at all this stuff!" Woody walked across the top of a display cabinet, admiring all the different *Woody's Roundup* collectibles. Soon Jessie and Bullseye joined him.

"Didn't you know? Why, you're valuable property," said Jessie.

"Oh, I wish the guys could see this. Hey howdy hey, that's me! I'm on a yo-yo!" Woody said, picking up a yo-yo with his face on it and giving it a spin. Next he walked over to a game labeled WOODY'S BALL TOSS and threw a ball, knocking a tooth out of a picture of himself. He put some coins in the Roundup bank, then began pumping a bubble machine. "What . . . you push the hat, and out comes . . . Oh, out come bubbles! Clever." Woody was getting used to the idea of being the star of his own TV show. In fact, he was beginning to like it.

Jessie and the Prospector laughed as Bullseye began popping the bubbles with his mouth as they came out. Woody continued to explore, examining a large boot on the shelf. He stepped on the spur on the boot's heel, and a spring snake jumped out, smacking him in the face. "Ah-ha-ha, I get it! There's a snake in my boot." He picked up the boot and pointed it down the shelf. "Bullseye—go long!" he called before firing the snake into the air.

Bullseye ran after it and happily leaped into the air, missing the snake but landing on a *Woody's Roundup* record player. It turned on and began cranking out old Western music, spinning Bullseye around and around as it played. Woody and Jessie jumped on the record player with him, and all three toys began to dance. Woody made a game of jumping up to avoid the arm, and Jessie joined him, hopping in time to the music.

"Not bad," said Woody. Then he turned up the speed of the record player, and Jessie, Bullseye, and Woody all began laughing and racing to keep up.

"Whooo-eee!" shouted Jessie. "Look at us! We're a complete set!"

"Now it's on to the museum!" said the Prospector.

"Museum?" asked Woody. He stopped short, causing all of them to trip over the arm of the record player. Jessie shrieked as they flew across the room and landed in a heap on the shelf. "What museum?" asked Woody, confused.

"We're being sold to the Konishi Toy Museum in Tokyo," explained the Prospector excitedly.

"That's in Japan!" added Jessie.

"Japan? I can't go to Japan," said Woody, standing up and brushing the dust from his knees.

"What do you mean?" asked Jessie, straightening her braid.

"I've got to get back home to my owner, Andy! Look, see?" Woody raised his boot and pointed to the name ANDY written on its sole.

"He still has an owner!" gasped Jessie.

"Oh, my goodness," said the Prospector, scratching his head.

"I can't do storage again. I won't go back in the dark," Jessie declared nervously, starting to hyperventilate.

"Jessie!" cried the Prospector as the cowgirl moaned frantically.

"What's the matter? What's wrong with her?" asked Woody.

The Prospector turned to Woody. "Well, we've been in storage for a long time," he explained. "Waiting for you."

"Why me?" asked Woody.

"The museum's only interested in the collection if you're in it, Woody. Without you, we go back into storage. It's that simple."

"It's not fair!" cried Jessie. "How can you do this to us?"

"Hey, look." Woody put his arms up and backed away. "I'm sorry, but this is all a big mistake. See, I was in this yard sale and—"

"Yard sale?" said the Prospector. "Why were you in a yard sale if you have an owner?"

"Well, I wasn't supposed to be there," Woody explained. "I was trying to save another toy, and—"

"Was it because you're damaged? Did this *Andy* break you?" asked the Prospector.

Woody cradled his broken arm defensively. "Yes, but . . . No, no, no! It was an accident. I mean—"

"Sounds like he *really* loves you," snapped Jessie sarcastically.

"It's not like that, okay?" shouted Woody. "And I'm not going to any museum!"

"Well, I'm not going back into storage!" Jessie shouted right back.

Suddenly, the apartment door creaked open. "Al's coming!" warned the Prospector. The Roundup gang scrambled to their packing boxes.

But Jessie couldn't bring herself to jump in.

"Jessie, I promise you'll come out of the box. Now go!" urged the Prospector. Jessie finally jumped in. Bullseye and the Prospector followed as Woody ran back to his glass case.

Seconds later, Al entered the room, carrying a camera. "It's showtime!" he said with a laugh. He pulled Bullseye and Jessie out of their box and arranged them in front of a cardboard Roundup barn for a photo. "Money, money, money," he said to himself with a chuckle. "And now, the main attraction." He grabbed Woody from his case, but a thread from Woody's torn shoulder caught on his display stand. As Al pulled Woody away, Woody's arm ripped off completely and fell to the floor. "Aaaaah!" yelled Al, finally noticing. "His arm! Where's his arm?"

Al found the arm on the ground, grabbed it, and tried to reattach it to Woody's shoulder. "What am I going to do?" he cried hysterically. "Oh, I know, I know." Al dropped Woody and reached for the phone, dialing with desperation.

"It's me—Al. I got an emergency here!" he barked into the phone. "It *has* to be tonight! All right, all right. But first thing in the morning!" Al slammed down the phone and stomped out of the room.

"It's gone!" said Woody, horrified. "I can't believe it. My arm is completely gone!"

"Come here," said the Prospector. "Let me see that. Oh, it's just a popped seam. You should consider yourself lucky."

"Lucky! Are you shrink-wrapped?" said Woody. "I am missing my arm!"

Jessie sat on the display cabinet and frowned. "Let him go. I'm sure his precious Andy is dying to play with a one-armed cowboy doll."

"Why, Jessie," replied the Prospector, "you know he wouldn't last an hour on the streets in his condition. It's a dangerous world out there for a toy."

Chapter

Buzz leaped out of a pile of shrubs, ran down the sidewalk, and took cover behind a mailbox. The night sky was dark, but the toys still had to be careful that no one saw them. Buzz looked back and motioned for the other toys to follow him.

Rex jumped out of the shrubs first, camouflaged in a bundle of leaves. As he ran toward Buzz, all but one of the leaves fell away. He laughed nervously, realizing his cover had been blown.

Slinky and Hamm appeared next, scurrying along quickly. Hamm tripped over a crack and his cork popped out, sending a handful of coins clanging to the ground. "All right, nobody look till I get my cork back in!" he cried.

Buzz stared down at the map he'd made earlier from Etch's drawing. "Good work, men. Two blocks down and only nineteen more to go," he said.

"Nineteen!" cried the other toys.

Buzz waved his arm to quiet them. "Come on, fellas. Did Woody give up when Sid had me strapped to a rocket?"

"No," said the others.

"No!" chimed Buzz. "We have a friend in need, and we will not rest until he's safe in Andy's room. Now, let's move out!" Buzz marched down the street, and the other toys followed.

A loud snoring sound rumbled through Al's apartment. From his glass case, Woody watched as Al slept on the couch, the TV blaring static in the background. Al's arm fell to the ground, dropping a bowl of cheese puffs and scattering them all over the floor. Woody could see his own broken arm in Al's shirt pocket. Now was his chance!

Woody pushed open the glass case with a quiet *creak* and hopped down to the floor. Suddenly— *crunch!*—Woody looked down to find that he had stepped on one of Al's cheese puffs. Not wanting to wake Al, Woody tiptoed across the floor, being careful to avoid stepping on another cheese puff.

Crunch! Woody turned to find Bullseye standing on a crushed cheese puff, wagging his tail excitedly.

"Bullseye, go!" Woody whispered. "Come on, you don't want to help me! Now just go!"

Bullseye responded by giving Woody's face a big lick.

"All right," conceded Woody. "But you have *got* to keep quiet."

Bullseye nodded.

Woody quietly led Bullseye over to Al. When they reached the couch, Bullseye crouched down and allowed Woody to climb onto his back like a stepladder.

"Okay, Bullseye. Upsy-daisy," whispered Woody. Bullseye stood, raising Woody so that he was level with Al's head. Woody climbed onto the couch near Al's shoulder and stretched to reach his arm into Al's pocket. But it was too far away. Carefully, Woody tiptoed onto Al's chest and leaned toward the shirt pocket.

Suddenly, Al began to chuckle in his sleep. Woody looked down to find Bullseye licking cheese from Al's fingers.

"Stop it, Bullseye!" cried Woody in a loud whisper. Bullseye stopped, and Woody continued to creep across Al's chest. Just as he reached the shirt pocket and began to slide his arm out, Al's stomach gurgled, and a large belch escaped from his lips.

Woody began to gag. He waved his hat around to try to get rid of the terrible odor. Then, holding his breath, he grabbed his arm out of Al's shirt pocket and began to retreat across Al's chest.

Woody was nearly safe when the TV suddenly began to blast an episode of *Woody's Roundup*. Woody froze, wide-eyed, and then went flying to one side as a startled Al jumped up.

"Ahhhh!" Al cried when he spotted Woody lying on the floor below him, his broken arm beside him. He picked Woody up and put him back in the case. "Get in there. Cheap case," he muttered. "Now, where is the remote?" Woody looked over to see the remote sitting suspiciously in front of Jessie's case. She must have been responsible for waking Al!

Al picked up the remote and turned the TV off, then left the room carrying Woody's arm. As the door closed behind Al, Woody pushed open his case and marched over to Jessie.

"What is your problem?" he asked angrily. "Look, I'm sorry I can't help you guys out. But you didn't have to go and pull a stunt like that!"

"You think *I* did that?" replied Jessie.

"Oh, right. The TV just *happened* to turn on and the remote *magically* ended up in front of you!" said Woody.

"You calling me a liar?" asked Jessie.

"Well, if the boot fits," said Woody indignantly. Jessie's eye began to twitch with anger. She slowly reached up and pulled her hat down tightly. Sensing trouble, Bullseye jumped out of his case and hid in a nearby cookie jar.

"Okay, cowboy," said Jessie. She kicked open the door of her case. With a yell, she leaped from the case, landing on Woody and pinning him to the ground. She began to twist his only arm. "Take it back!" she cried. "Take it back!"

"Don't think just because you're a girl, I'm gonna take it easy on you!" shouted Woody as he struggled to free himself.

"Jessie! Woody! You stop this at once," the Prospector called suddenly. The wrestling toys looked up to see the Prospector's box on the shelf above them. He rocked his box back and forth as he tried to get Jessie's and Woody's attention, but suddenly, the box fell face-forward onto the cabinet. With a horrified gasp, Bullseye and Jessie rushed to help him.

"I don't know how that television show turned on, but fighting about it isn't helping anything," the Prospector told them sternly.

"If I had both my arms . . . ," Woody growled in Jessie's direction.

"Well, the fact is, you don't, Woody!" snapped the Prospector. "So I suggest you just wait until morning. The Cleaner will come, fix your arm, and—"

"And then I'm out of here," finished Woody. Bullseye looked up, a hurt expression on his face. Jessie scowled at Woody as she tried to comfort the sad little horse. "Oh, no, Bullseye—don't take it that way," Woody tried to explain. "It's just that Andy—"

"Andy! Andy! Andy! That's all he ever talks about!" cried Jessie. She turned and walked away, and Bullseye followed. Woody watched them sadly.

The sun rose as Buzz and his rescue party made their way through a group of hedges. Buzz was in the lead, karate-chopping a path through the leaves.

"Hey, Buzz, can we slow down?" asked Hamm. "May I remind you that some of us are carrying over six dollars in change?"

"Losing health units . . . must rest," panted Rex.

Buzz stopped and waited for the other toys to catch up to him. "Is everyone present and accounted for?" he asked.

"Not quite everyone," someone chimed.

"Who's behind?" asked Buzz.

"Mine," said Slinky, whose rear end was trailing far behind. The group waited while Slinky's back legs tiredly caught up with everyone else.

"Hey, guys!" said Hamm, looking out from the bushes. "Why do the toys cross the road?"

"Not now, Hamm," said Buzz.

"Ooh! I love riddles. Why?" asked Rex.

"To get to the chicken *on the other side*!" Hamm answered. He pointed. Al's Toy Barn was directly across the street. A giant statue of a chicken loomed in front of the buildng.

"Hooray! The chicken!" shouted Rex. Everyone whooped with excitement.

Suddenly, the honking of horns made them realize that there was a busy two-way street between them and Al's Toy Barn. A truck rumbled by, shooting a crushed soda can toward the toys. They ducked and scrambled out of the way.

"Oh, well. We tried," said Rex, inching away from the street.

Buzz grabbed him by the tail. "We'll have to cross," he said.

"I may not be a smart dog," said Slinky. "But I know what roadkill is!"

"There must be a safe way," Buzz insisted. His eyes narrowed as he studied the street scene.

Moments later, Buzz had worked out a plan. Construction workers had left a pile of orange traffic cones at the edge of the street, and each one was the perfect size to hide a toy. Soon the entire rescue party was standing under the cones, completely hidden from sight.

"Okay, here's our chance! Ready . . . set . . . go!" ordered Buzz.

The cones began to move, wobbling slowly

across the street. For a moment, the street was empty. Then the traffic light turned green and a stream of cars sped toward them. "Drop!" yelled Buzz. All of the cones dropped to the ground, looking like ordinary traffic cones. "Go!" he shouted when it was clear. The toys did their best to hurry forward, but it was slow going. All around them, cars veered and screeched out of their way, honking and even smashing into each other.

But before long, the toys had arrived safely on the other side of the street.

"Good job, troops," said Buzz. "We're that much closer to Woody!"

Chapter

Back in Al's apartment, Woody heard the doorbell ring. Al opened the door to reveal the Cleaner, a little old man carrying a large case that resembled a doctor's bag.

"Is the specimen ready for cleaning?" the Cleaner asked Al. He slammed his case down on a table and opened it. On the left side was a foldout shelf full of all kinds of tools. On the right side was a little cabinet with an air compressor inside. The Cleaner pressed a button and a miniature hat rack popped up. He took Woody's hat and hung it on one of the hooks. Then he gently placed Woody in a vise that looked like a tiny dentist's chair, and began to examine the toy closely.

Woody has been shelved in Andy's room.

When Woody is toynapped by an evil toy collector named Al, Buzz races to the rescue.

Woody meets Jessie the cowgirl at Al's apartment.

The Prospector and Bullseye the horse introduce themselves to Woody.

Woody discovers that he is part of the Roundup gang.

The Prospector explains that the Roundup gang is on its way to a toy museum—in Japan!

Buzz leads Andy's toys on a rescue mission to Al's Toy Barn.

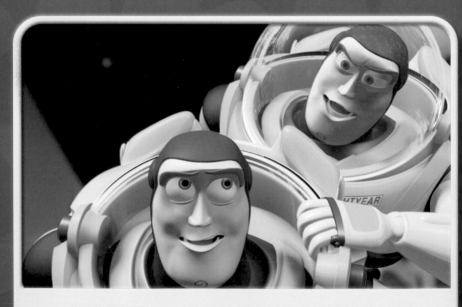

Buzz is captured by . . . *himself*?

Woody plans his escape from Al's apartment.

"Ride like the wind, Bullseye!"

Woody's rescuers arrive!

"I'm the real Buzz!"

The Prospector is out of his box!

Oh, no—it's Emperor Zurg!

Woody and Jessie attempt a daring escape.

The toys are safe and sound!

"How long is this going to take?" asked Al impatiently.

"You can't rush art," replied the Cleaner. He dipped a cotton swab into a cleaning solution and began to wipe Woody's eyes and ears. He then used the air compressor to spray paint onto Woody's cheeks and over a worn spot on his head.

Next he pulled out his strongest magnifying lens and positioned it in front of Woody. Then he threaded a needle and began to stitch Woody's arm into place. A few minutes later, Woody's arm was back where it belonged.

The Cleaner used a tiny rag to shine Woody's boots. Then he picked up one boot and applied a coat of paint to the sole, covering Andy's name. He positioned Woody carefully back in his case and then, with a satisfied chuckle, placed Woody's hat on his head.

"He's for display only," warned the Cleaner. "You handle him too much, he's not going to last."

"You're a genius!" cried Al. "Oh, he's just like new!"

Meanwhile, Buzz and his rescue party were almost at Al's Toy Barn. When they got to the building, they noticed a large sign on the door.

"Oh, no. It's closed!" cried Slinky.

Suddenly, a workman approached. The toys hid under a shopping cart and watched as he stepped on the black mat in front of the store. Automatic doors slid open and he walked inside.

"Hey, Joe, you're late! We've got a ton of toys to unload," called another workman from inside the store.

"All right, I'm coming," replied Joe.

The toys glanced at each other. Buzz nodded. "All right, let's go!" he ordered.

"But the sign says it's closed," said Rex. Everyone ignored him and began jumping crazily on the black doormat.

But still the doors stayed closed.

"No, no, no," said Buzz. "All together." Everyone paused, and then Buzz yelled, "Now!" All the toys jumped at once. When they landed on the mat, the doors whooshed open and they stepped inside.

Al's Toy Barn was huge. Thousands of toys lined the walls, stretching into the distance. Rex was quickly distracted by a display of books at the front entrance. He giggled excitedly when he saw the cover of a video game strategy guide: *Want to DEFEAT ZURG? Secrets revealed!* But the other toys felt overwhelmed. "Whoa, Nellie! How are we going to find Woody in this place?" asked Slinky.

"Look for Al," directed Buzz. "We find Al, we find Woody. Now, move out!" The toys scattered in search of Woody.

As Buzz turned a corner, he came face to face with an entire aisle of Buzz Lightyear action figure boxes. He stared in awe. "Wow." He stepped forward to examine the toys more closely. A bright green glow captured his attention, and he noticed a special display with a sign that read NEW UTILITY BELT.

"I could use one of those," marveled Buzz. He climbed to the top of the display case and looked around. Right in front of him was a pair of moon boots. He glanced up. Towering over him was a new Buzz Lightyear toy.

Buzz circled the New Buzz, sizing him up. The action figure stood frozen in place, unblinking. Buzz checked out his reflection in New Buzz's shiny clear helmet. "Am I really that fat?" he wondered aloud. Then Buzz spied the figure's utility belt and whistled in appreciation. Slowly, he reached for it.

"Ho-yahhh!" yelled New Buzz, suddenly grabbing Buzz's arm. Swiftly, he pinned Buzz's arm behind his back.

"Oww! What are you doing?" complained Buzz.

"You're in direct violation of code six-four-oh-four-point-five, stating all space rangers are to be in hypersleep until awakened by authorized personnel!" barked New Buzz in a stiff, computerlike voice. He pointed toward all the other Buzz Lightyears that still stood motionless in their boxes.

"Oh, no," said Buzz in exasperation.

New Buzz spun Buzz around, pushing him up against the display. "You're breaking ranks, Ranger," he said. New Buzz kicked Buzz's legs apart and twisted his arms behind his back. Then New Buzz opened his wrist communicator. "Buzz Lightyear to Star Command. I've got an AWOL space ranger."

"Tell me I wasn't this deluded," Buzz said, rolling his eyes.

"No back talk," warned New Buzz. "I have a laser, and I will use it."

"You mean the laser that's a lightbulb?" teased Buzz as he pressed the button.

New Buzz gasped and leaped out of the way. "Has your mind been melded? You could've killed me, Space Ranger. Or should I say 'Traitor'?"

Buzz broke free. "I don't have time for this," he said, walking away.

New Buzz raised his laser and aimed it at Buzz's head. "Halt! I order you to halt!"

Buzz dropped from the display case to the floor. But New Buzz followed and tackled him. The two began to wrestle. Finally, New Buzz managed to shove Buzz into an empty box, using the packaging wires to secure him inside.

"Ow!" said Buzz, his voice muffled by layers of packaging. "Listen to me! You're not really a space ranger! You're a toy! We're all toys! Do you hear me?"

New Buzz closed the cardboard box and placed it back on the shelf. "Well, that should hold you until the court-martial!"

"You don't realize what you're doing!" Buzz pleaded from the box.

Meanwhile, the rest of the toys were exploring a different aisle. Rex was still reading his *Defeat Zurg* strategy book, and Hamm had found a blue toy sports car. Rex, Hamm, and Slinky drove off, ramming into an occasional shelf or display.

Rex, sitting in back, continued to read from his manual. "Aaaahh! It says how you defeat Zurg! Look!" He placed the book in front of the windshield so that everyone could read. But now no one could see where they were going. The car swerved, and the toys screamed.

"Look out!" yelled Slinky. The car was headed directly for a giant box of rubber balls.

The car hit the side of the box and the balls spilled out, cascading to the ground in a blizzard of multicolored rubber. Balls bounced off everything, including the car. Everyone yelled as the car spun around wildly.

Rex's manual flew out into the aisle. "My source of power!" he yelled, jumping out of the car and racing after the book. It slid under a shelf, lost. "No! Come back!" Then Rex looked up to see the car speeding away. "Wait up! Dinosaur overboard!" he called as he began to chase after the car.

The car swerved down the Buzz Lightyear

aisle just as New Buzz turned to walk away from Buzz, now secure in his box on the shelf. The other toys pulled up to New Buzz.

"Hey, Buzz," said Hamm.

New Buzz turned, took aim, and fired his laser at the toys. "Halt!" he shouted. "Who goes there?"

The toys were amused by what they thought was Buzz's joke. "Buzz! I know how to defeat Zurg!" said Rex.

Suddenly, New Buzz's attitude changed. "You do?" he asked.

"C'mon, I'll tell you on the way," said Rex.

The real Buzz watched from the shelf, horrified. "No, no, guys! You've got the wrong Buzz!"

"Say, where'd you get the cool belt, Buzz?" asked Hamm.

"Well, slotted pig, they're standard-issue," said New Buzz. He jumped into the car and the whole group drove away.

"Noooo!" Buzz yelled from inside the box. But no one could hear him.

Chapter

A flash went off, blinding Woody momentarily. He was propped up on a stand, posed with the rest of the Roundup gang. *Flash! Flash! Flash!*

Al fanned through his new photos with a huge smile on his face. "It's like printing my own money!" he exclaimed. The phone rang and Al picked it up. "Yeah, what?" he shouted. Then his voice turned respectful. "Oh, Mr. Konishi. I have the pictures right here. In fact, I'm in the car right now, on my way to the office to fax them to you. I'm going through a tunnel," he lied. "I'm breaking up." He made some garbled sounds and then hung up the phone and left the room.

As soon as Al was gone, Woody leaped from his stand. "Oh, wow! Will you look at me! It's like

I'm fresh out of the box!" Woody admired his repaired arm. "Look at this stitching! Andy's going to have a hard time ripping this!" He waved his new arm wildly in front of the other toys' faces. "Hello! Hi! Hello!"

Woody used the cellophane front of the Prospector's box to check his reflection. Jessie frowned and walked away. "Great, now you can go," she said before storming off in a huff.

"Well, what a good idea," said Woody. He walked toward the heating vent. Then he paused, thinking. Bullseye came up and nudged him from behind. Woody stared into the horse's sad eyes.

"Woody, don't be mad at Jessie," said the Prospector. "She's been through more than you know. Why not make amends before you leave, huh? It's the least you can do."

Woody sighed and looked over at Jessie, who was sitting on the window ledge. "All right. But I don't know what good it'll do." He climbed onto a chair and stood just below Jessie. "Hey, whatcha doing way up here?"

Jessie hugged her knees to her chest and stared out the window, avoiding eye contact with Woody. "I thought I'd get one last look at the sun before I get packed away again," she said.

"Look, Jessie, I know you hate me for leaving, but I have to go back. I'm still Andy's toy. Well, if you knew him, you'd understand. You see, Andy's a real—"

"Let me guess," Jessie interrupted. "Andy's a real special kid, and to him you're his buddy, his best friend. And when Andy plays with you, it's like, even though you're not moving, you feel like you're alive—because that's how he sees you."

Woody was stunned. "How did you know that?" he asked.

Jessie stared at Woody. "Because Emily was just the same. She was my whole world." Jessie explained that she had had an owner once, too. Emily had loved Jessie just like Andy loved

Woody. And Jessie had loved Emily right back. But then Emily grew up and gave Jessie away. "You never forget kids like Emily, or Andy. But they forget you," Jessie said sadly.

"Jessie, I . . . I didn't know," said Woody, stunned.

"Just go," she said.

Woody reluctantly slid to the floor and walked slowly over to the heating vent. He opened the grate and stood quietly in front of it for a moment, staring down the ventilation shaft.

"How long will it last, Woody?" asked the Prospector. "Do you really think Andy is going to take you to college? Or on his honeymoon? Andy's growing up, and there's nothing you can do about it." Woody listened silently, a sad expression growing on his face as he began to hear the truth in the Prospector's words. "It's your choice, Woody. You can go back, or you can stay with us and last forever. You'll be adored by children for generations."

As Woody stood thinking, Bullseye came over

and gazed woefully up at the cowboy. Finally, Woody made a decision. "Who am I to break up the Roundup gang?" he asked. He looked back at Jessie, and the two exchanged a smile.

Back at Al's Toy Barn, the rescue party had made it to Al's office. The toys rummaged through desk drawers and opened boxes, searching for clues.

"Woody! Woody!" they called frantically.

Off to one side, Rex was talking to New Buzz. Rex was still excited about what he'd learned from the video game strategy book. "You see, all along we thought that the way into Zurg's fortress was through the main gate. But in fact, the secret entrance is to the left, hidden in the shadows."

New Buzz nodded. "To the left and in the shadows. Got it."

Suddenly, they heard footsteps in the hall. "Someone's coming!" cried Slinky. The toys hid under the desk as Al entered the office, turning on his fax machine as he talked into his cell phone. "Now, let me confirm your fax number. Wait, that's a lot of numbers. . . . No, I got it."

"It's him," whispered Slinky.

"The chicken man!" said Hamm.

"Funny, he doesn't look like poultry," said New Buzz.

"That's the kidnapper, all right," said Slinky.

"A kidnapper," said New Buzz. "An agent of Zurg if I ever saw one."

"And the pièce de résistance," Al said into the phone as he slid a photo of Woody through the fax machine. "I promise the collection will be the crown jewel of your museum!" The photo went through the machine and popped out the other side, falling to the floor near the toys.

"It's Woody!" gasped Slinky.

"Now that I have your attention, imagine we added another zero to the price, huh? What? Yes? Yes! You've got a deal!" Al yelled. "I'll be on the next flight to Japan!"

New Buzz pushed everyone into Al's bag.

"Quick! Into the poultry man's cargo unit. He'll lead us to Zurg. Move, move, move!"

Al began to laugh. "Al, you are gonna be rich! Rich! Rich!" he bellowed, picking up his bag. He didn't notice Rex's tail hanging out the back—or any of the other toys who had sneaked inside.

Inside the toy store, Buzz had managed to shift his box sideways on the shelf. With each shove against the plastic front, he moved another inch. He teetered over the edge and finally dropped to the floor. He kicked open the bottom of the box, then struggled with the arm restraints. He jerked his right arm hard and broke free, then untied the rest of his body and crawled out of the box.

Suddenly, Buzz heard Al whooping and laughing as he walked down a nearby aisle. Peering around the corner, Buzz saw Al carrying a bag—and Rex's tail was sticking out of it! Buzz raced down a parallel aisle, trying to catch up to his friends. He was almost in the clear when he slipped on some loose balls left over from Hamm's car crash. Buzz recovered quickly and climbed up a display case. Swinging like a gymnast, he leaped onto a trampoline, then bounced up to grab a toy on a wire. Al was heading for the front door, and Buzz was desperate to follow him.

Sliding down the wire, Buzz let go of the toy and dove for the closing electric doors . . . and smacked right into them as they shut. "Oof!" he yelled. He jumped up and down on the doormat sensor, but the door wouldn't budge. He watched in frustration as Al got into his car and drove away. Luckily, the car didn't go far—it parked in front of a high-rise apartment building just across the street.

Buzz looked around and spotted a large display of boxes by the door. He kicked the bottom box out of the stack, causing the entire pile to topple over. The weight of the boxes made the door open, and Buzz ran through it, chasing Al.

Behind him, Buzz didn't notice that one of the boxes was caught between the electronic doors.

Over and over, the doors opened and shut, jarring the box. Finally, a large black hand punched out from the top. Then a frightening purple figure emerged. It was an Emperor Zurg toy! Zurg sat up and whipped his head toward Buzz. His red eyes glowed and his claws clenched as his Zurg-o-vision finder set its sights on the space ranger. Zurg's deep mechanical voice growled, "Destroy Buzz Lightyear! Destroy Buzz Lightyear!" Freed from his box, Zurg set off on Buzz's trail.

Chapter

From inside Al's bag, the toys heard Al cut the engine. He got out of the car and slammed the door behind him.

"He didn't take the bag!" said Rex from inside.

New Buzz hopped over Rex and jumped out of the bag. "No time to lose," the space ranger said. He tried the door handle, but it wouldn't open.

Peering through the car window, the toys watched Al enter the building and get into the elevator. "He's ascending in the vertical transporter," said New Buzz, opening his wings. "All right, everyone! Hang on! We're going to blast through the roof!"

"Uh, Buzz . . . ," said Rex.

"To infinity . . . and beyond!" boomed New

Buzz. The other toys just stared at him. As they worked to pop open the door lock, New Buzz kept trying to blast through the roof. He scratched his head. "I don't understand. Somehow my fuel cells have gone dry."

New Buzz accidentally leaned against the Unlock button, and the lock suddenly popped up. The car door opened and New Buzz ran to the front door of the building. He watched through the glass doors as the elevator needle stopped at the twenty-third floor.

"Blast!" cried New Buzz. "He's on level twenty-three."

"How are we gonna get up there?" asked Slinky.

Rex looked up. "Maybe if we find some balloons, we could float to the top."

"Troops! Over here," called New Buzz. They all turned to see him taking the cover off an air vent. "Just like you said, Lizard Man—in the shadows, to the left. Okay, let's move!"

The toys followed New Buzz into the duct. He

spoke into his wrist communicator. "Mission Log: have infiltrated enemy territory without detection and are making our way through the bowels of Zurg's fortress."

Hamm turned to the others. "You know, I think that Buzz aisle went to his head," he whispered. The others nodded, but they all followed New Buzz through the shaft.

Soon they came to an intersection with another duct. Slinky looked in both directions. "Oh, no. Which way do we go?" he asked.

"This way," said New Buzz, running forward. Then a noise echoed through the duct. "We've been detected!" cried New Buzz. "The walls! They're closing in!"

"Guys, look! It's not the walls, it's the elevator," said Rex. He pointed to a different duct, where they could see the elevator heading down.

They walked to the elevator shaft and peered up. "Come on," New Buzz said. "We've got no time to lose." He put on a pair of suction-cup gloves and reeled out a line and hook. "Everyone grab hold."

"Huh?" asked the others.

"Uh, Buzz?" asked Hamm. "Why don't we just take the elevator?"

New Buzz began to scale the walls with his suction-cup gloves. "They'll be expecting that," he explained.

Meanwhile, an orange traffic cone made its way to the entrance of Al's building. A weary and frustrated Buzz peeked out from underneath. He noticed a trail of footprints in the soft grass, leading to the vent. He hid beneath the cone once again and followed the trail.

Inside his apartment, Al was pacing back and forth in the living room, yelling into his phone.

"I'll have the stuff waiting in the lobby, and you'd better be here in fifteen minutes, because I have a plane to catch. Do you hear me?"

On the floor, the Roundup gang was packed into special foam trays. They weren't being shipped to Japan—they were going on the plane with Al in a green metal suitcase. When Al left the apartment, Woody, Jessie, and Bullseye sat up in their trays.

"Woo-hoo!" yelled Jessie. "We're finally going! Can you believe it?"

Bullseye excitedly sniffed his thick foam packaging.

The Prospector chuckled. "That's custom-fitted foam insulation you'll be riding in, Bullseye. First-class all the way!"

"You know what?" said Woody. "I'm actually excited about this. I mean it. I really am!"

Jessie jumped next to Woody, and they began to square dance. "Yee-haw! Swing yer partner, do-si-do! Look at you, dancin' cowboy!" she said.

Bullseye began to chase his tail as the Prospector rocked his box back and forth. "Look! I'm doing the box step!" he cried.

Back in the elevator shaft, New Buzz climbed slowly, pulling the others behind him. Hamm grunted. He tilted, and some of his change began to drop out of his coin slot. "Uh-oh. Hey, heads up down there!" he called.

"Whoa! Pork bellies are falling," said Slinky.

"My arms can't hold on much longer," complained Rex as he began to slide down New Buzz's towline. Rex bumped into the other toys and pushed them down with him. They all clung desperately to the end of the towline.

"Too . . . heavy," panted New Buzz. Suddenly, he got an idea. "What was I thinking? My antigravity servos!" He pushed a button on his utility belt.

"Hang tight, everyone," said New Buzz. "I'm going to let go of the wall."

"What?" the toys cried.

"One . . . ," called New Buzz. "Two . . ."

"No, Buzz!" exclaimed the toys. "No, don't—"

"Three!" shouted New Buzz. He pushed off the wall and went into his flying pose, one fist jutting forward. The toys stayed frozen in space for a second. Then they began to plummet. Luckily, they landed on top of the rising elevator after only a short drop.

"To infinity . . . and beyond!" called New Buzz, unaware that his attempt at flying had failed. The elevator began to slow down. "Approaching destination. Reengaging gravity," New Buzz said. The others looked at each other and rolled their eyes. The elevator stopped right at the air vent on the twenty-third floor. New Buzz leaped into the vent and scanned it for danger. "Area secure," he reported to the others. They groaned and panted as they climbed into the vent.

"It's okay, troops. The antigravity sickness will wear off momentarily. Now . . . let's move!" said New Buzz.

As they followed New Buzz through the vent, none of the toys realized that the *real* Buzz was clinging to the bottom of the elevator, determined to find Woody and reunite with his friends.

Chapter

In Al's apartment, Woody was having fun playing with his new friends. They had propped a packing box on its side, turning it into a makeshift saloon.

"How 'bout givin' me a little intro there, Jessie?" called Woody from inside the box.

Jessie began, "Introducing the high-ridin'est cowboy around—"

"You forgot rootin'-tootin'est!" said Woody.

"The high-ridin'est, rootin'-tootin'est cowboy hero of all time . . . Sheriff Woody!" announced Jessie.

Woody strolled out through the box flaps as though they were saloon doors. With smooth confidence, he swaggered over to Jessie. "Say, little missy," he said, "you notice any trouble around these parts?"

"Nary a bit," replied Jessie. "Not with Sheriff Woody around."

Then Woody had an idea. "Wait! I got it!" he exclaimed. "Okay, the bandits got the critters tied up in the burning barn, and now for the best part!" He ran over to the packing box excitedly and jumped inside, calling, "Help us! The barn's on fire!" in the voice of the trapped critters. Then he popped out of the box holding an armful of packing peanuts.

"I've gotcha, critters! No need to worry," he said. "Woody saves the day again!"

"Yee-haw!" shouted Jessie.

"Now, where's my trusty steed, Bullseye?" asked Woody. "I have to ride off into the sunset."

An eager Bullseye galloped over to Woody, picking him up in one swift move. The pair struck a gallant pose. Then Woody shouted, "Ride like the wind, Bullseye!"

Bullseye reared up, preparing to run. Suddenly,

Woody slid right off the horse's back, along with the saddle! "Whoa—oof!" Woody groaned as he landed on the floor in a pile. Jessie grabbed him under the arms to help him up.

"Wait! I'm ticklish, okay?" cried Woody.

"Oh, you are?" asked Jessie playfully. She and Bullseye pounced on Woody and began to tickle him.

"No, no, please!" cried Woody between bursts of laughter. "Stop it! Please! Stop!"

Inside the air vent that led to Al's apartment, New Buzz spoke into his wrist communicator again. "Mission Log: have reached Zurg's command deck, but no sign of him, or his wooden captive."

Suddenly, Woody's voice echoed through the chambers. "Please! No! Stop!"

"That's Woody!" said Slinky before letting out a howl.

"This way!" cried New Buzz.

The toys turned and ran down the duct. They reached the grate that opened into Al's apartment and tried to peer through. They could hear Woody's voice, but they couldn't see him. "I'm begging you! No more! I'm begging you, stop!" Woody pleaded as Jessie continued to tickle him.

"They're torturing him!" cried the toys.

Rex gasped. "What are we going to do, Buzz?" he asked.

"Use your head," said New Buzz.

The toys grabbed Rex and aimed his head at the grate. Using him as a battering ram, they scrambled forward. "But I don't want to use my head!" cried Rex.

"Charge!" the rest of the toys yelled, running full-speed toward the grate. Woody hadn't screwed the grate back onto the vent, and it gave way as soon as the toys hit it. They crashed into Al's apartment, passing the Roundup gang and smashing into the far wall.

Woody, Jessie, Bullseye, and the Prospector froze, shocked by the sudden arrival.

"What's going on here?" asked the Prospector.

"Guys!" cried Woody. "How did you find me?"

"Watch yourself!" shouted New Buzz. Then he pushed Woody to the ground in an effort to protect him, while Andy's toys rushed the Roundup gang.

"We're here to spring you, Woody," explained Slinky.

Hamm tackled the Prospector, knocking his box flat on its back. "You heard of kung fu?" Hamm shouted. "Well, get ready for pork chop!"

"Hold it!" cried Woody. "Hey, you don't understand! These are my friends."

"Yeah, we're his friends," said Rex.

"No, Rex. I mean *they're* my friends," said Woody, pointing at the Roundup gang. Slinky and Bullseye began to circle one another, snarling. Slinky's coil arched like a cat about to fight. Jessie ran over to try to break them up, and Slinky quickly tied her and Bullseye up with his coils.

"Hey!" cried Jessie.

"Grab Woody and let's go!" ordered Slinky. New Buzz ran to Woody, picked him up, and started to carry him off.

"Fellas, hold it!" Woody protested. "Hey, Buzz—put me down!"

"Quick, to the vent!" Andy's toys shouted.

"They're stealing him!" cried Jessie in alarm.

"No!" shouted the Prospector.

The toys all rushed to the vent. Suddenly, the real Buzz blocked their path. "Hold it right there!" he said.

"Buzz?" said Woody and the rest of Andy's toys.

"You again?" asked New Buzz.

Buzz looked up at Woody, who was still in New Buzz's arms. "Woody! Thank goodness you're all right."

"Buzz, what is going on?" asked Woody.

New Buzz dropped Woody. "Hold on! I am Buzz Lightyear, and I'm in charge of this detachment."

"No, *I'm* Buzz Lightyear," Buzz told the others.

"So who's the real Buzz?" asked Woody.

"I am," both Buzzes replied.

New Buzz turned to the others. "Don't let this imposter fool you! He's been trained by Zurg himself to mimic my every move—"

Buzz reached over and popped New Buzz's helmet open. New Buzz sputtered and gasped for air, falling to the ground. As a newly woken space ranger, he still believed he was on a foreign planet and the air wasn't safe to breathe. While New Buzz faltered, Buzz calmly lifted his foot and showed everyone the ANDY written on the sole of his boot.

"Buzz!" cried Andy's other toys with relief.

"I had a feeling it was you, Buzz," said Slinky. "My front end just had to catch up with my back end."

New Buzz managed to close his helmet and stand up. "Will somebody please explain what's going on?" he asked, catching his breath.

"It's all right, Space Ranger," said Buzz. "It's a code five-forty-six."

New Buzz gasped. "You mean it's a—"

"Yes," said Buzz.

"And he's a—" said New Buzz.

"Oh, yeah," said Buzz.

New Buzz rushed over to Woody and bowed down on one knee. "Your Majesty," he said. Woody looked down, giggling in confusion.

Buzz took Woody's arm. "Woody, you're in danger here. We need to leave now."

"Al's selling you to a toy museum—in Japan!" cried Rex.

"I know. It's okay, Buzz," said Woody, pulling away. "I actually want to go."

"What?" cried Rex.

"The thing is," explained Woody, "I'm a rare Sheriff Woody doll, and these guys are my Roundup gang." He motioned to Jessie, Bullseye, and the Prospector, who all waved.

"Woody, what are you talking about?" asked Buzz.

"*Woody's Roundup*! It's this great old TV show, and I was the star!"

Woody clicked the remote, and the TV turned on and began to play an episode of *Woody's*

Roundup. "See, now look. Look at me! See, that's me!" said Woody.

On the screen, the TV Woody was riding the TV Bullseye. Andy's toys watched in confusion.

"This is weirdin' me out," said Hamm.

Woody explained, "Buzz, it was a national phenomenon! And there was all this merchandise that just got packed up. Oh, you should've seen it. There was a record player and a yo-yo. Buzz, I was a yo-yo!"

Buzz pulled Woody aside. "Woody, stop this nonsense and let's go."

"I can't go," said Woody with a sigh. "I can't abandon these guys. They need me to get into this museum. Without me they'll go back into storage—maybe forever."

Buzz raised his voice. "Woody, you're not a collector's item. You are a child's plaything. *You are a toy!*"

"For how much longer?" reasoned Woody. "One more rip, and Andy's done with me. What do I do then, Buzz, huh? You tell me."

"Somewhere in that pad of stuffing is a toy who taught me that life's only worth living if you're being loved by a kid," said Buzz. "And I traveled all this way to rescue that toy because I believed him."

"Well, you wasted your time," said Woody. He folded his arms and turned away from Buzz.

"Let's go, everyone," said Buzz.

"What about Woody?" asked Slinky.

"He's not coming with us," said Buzz as he turned toward the grate.

"But Andy's coming home tonight," said Rex.

"Then we'd better make sure we're there waiting for him," said Buzz.

Buzz waited by the vent as New Buzz and the rest of Andy's toys climbed through. Slinky glanced sadly at Woody before trudging out and disappearing into the darkness. Buzz paused, looking at Woody one last time.

"I don't have a choice, Buzz," said Woody, shrugging. "This is my only chance."

"To do what, Woody?" asked Buzz. "Watch kids from behind glass and never be loved again? Some life." He stepped into the vent and closed the grate behind him.

Chapter

Woody stared sadly at the closed grate.

"Good going, Woody. I thought they'd never leave," said the Prospector.

Woody didn't respond. Instead, he wandered over to the TV to watch the end of the *Woody's Roundup* episode that was still playing. The TV Woody was singing, and the song trickled through the grate, where Buzz paused to listen for a moment before turning away with a sigh.

On the TV screen, a shy little boy was pushed onto the stage. He slowly approached TV Woody. Then the boy hugged TV Woody with all his might.

Woody looked down at the sole of his boot. He scratched away the new paint until the name

ANDY showed through. He shook his head with a sigh and then stood up. "What am I doing?" he asked himself. Then he ran past the Roundup gang, heading straight for the vent.

"Buzz!" he called. "Wait!"

"Woody? Where are you going?" asked the Prospector nervously.

"You're right, Prospector. I can't stop Andy from growing up, but I wouldn't miss it for the world!"

"No!" said the Prospector with a gasp.

But Woody had already lifted the grate. "Buzz!" he yelled.

Inside the vent, both Buzzes turned. "Yes?" they asked.

"I'm coming with you!" shouted Woody. Andy's toys let out a cheer. Woody began to climb into the vent, but then stopped. He had an idea.

"Wait," said Woody. "I'll be back in just a second." He turned on his boot heel and ran back into Al's apartment. "Hey, you guys!" he called to the Roundup gang. "Come with me!"

"What?" asked Jessie in surprise.

"Andy will play with all of us, I know it," said Woody.

"Woody, I—I don't know . . . I . . . ," Jessie stammered.

"Wouldn't you give anything just to have one more day with Emily?" asked Woody. Jessie didn't know what to say. "C'mon, Jessie. This is what it's all about—to make a child happy. And you know it!" He turned to Bullseye. "Bullseye? Are you with me?"

Bullseye eagerly licked Woody's face.

"Good boy. Prospector, how about you?" Woody turned to the Prospector's box—but it was empty.

Suddenly, the toys heard a sharp clang. They spun around to see that the Prospector had slammed the grate shut and was using his plastic pick to tighten the screws.

Jessie gasped. "Prospector?"

"You're out of your box!" said Woody.

"I tried reasoning with you, Woody," said the

Prospector, "but you keep forcing me to take extreme measures." He finished tightening the screws and walked back to his box. He stopped at the TV remote and slammed his pick down on the Power button, turning off the *Woody's Roundup* episode.

"Wait a minute!" said Woody, a realization dawning on him. "*You* turned on the TV last night, not Jessie!"

"Look, we have an eternity to spend together in the museum," replied the Prospector. "Let's not start off by pointing fingers, shall we?"

"Prospector! This isn't fair," said Jessie.

"Fair?" asked the Prospector, raising his voice. "I'll tell you what's not *fair*: spending a lifetime on a dime-store shelf, watching every other toy be sold. Well, finally my waiting has paid off, and no hand-me-down cowboy doll is gonna mess it up for me now!" The Prospector flung his box into the special packing case.

Woody ran to the vent, pulling on the grate. "Buzz! Help! Guys!" he called.

"It's too late, Woody," said the Prospector. "That silly Buzz Lightweight can't help you."

"His name is Buzz Light*year*!" shouted Woody, struggling to open the grate.

"Whatever," said the Prospector. "I always hated those upstart space toys." He jumped into his box and closed the lid.

Bullseye joined Woody at the grate just as Andy's toys appeared on the other side. They all struggled to open it, but it wouldn't budge.

"It's stuck," said Woody. "What do we do?"

The two Buzzes began pulling on the grate. "Should I use my head?" offered Rex.

Suddenly, the lock on Al's apartment door began to rattle.

"It's Al!" cried Woody. Jessie and Bullseye jumped into their cases as the door creaked open. Woody had no choice but to fall limply to the floor.

Al burst into the apartment. "I'm gonna be late," he mumbled as he gathered up the Roundup toys and put them in the green suitcase before grabbing it and heading back out the door.

Andy's toys watched in horror as Woody was taken away. "Quick! To the elevator!" cried Buzz. The toys raced down the duct, both Buzzes leading the way.

"Hurry, I can hear it coming!" called Buzz. The toys rounded a corner and then stopped in their tracks.

Riding on top of the ascending elevator was Zurg. "So we meet again, Buzz Lightyear," he growled when he saw Buzz. The elevator came to a stop.

"It's Zurg!" yelled Rex. "Watch out, he's got an ion blaster!"

Zurg fired at New Buzz, who jumped into action. He leaped over Zurg and landed on top of the elevator. Then he aimed his laser at Zurg and fired.

"Ahhh!" cried Zurg. He continued firing his ion blaster at New Buzz, who moved swiftly to avoid the assault. The pair were engaged in heated combat as the elevator began to descend again.

"Quick, get on!" Buzz called to the rest of the toys. They jumped onto the elevator roof, where Buzz spotted the emergency panel.

"The emergency hatch! Come on!" Buzz shouted. He ran to the panel, motioning to the other toys to follow him.

Meanwhile, New Buzz continued to battle Zurg. *Pop! Pop! Pop!* Zurg fired his ion blaster— which really shot out Ping-Pong balls. New Buzz took cover behind a generator box, where he found several metal washers. He hurled them at Zurg, hitting him in the face.

"Ahhh!" Zurg cried. He grabbed New Buzz by the throat and began to bang his head against a metal fixture. Then Zurg lifted New Buzz over his head, spun him around, and threw him to the ground. New Buzz lay flat on his back as Zurg approached him menacingly.

"Surrender, Buzz Lightyear. I have won!" boomed Zurg.

"I'll never give in. You killed my father," said New Buzz.

"No, Buzz. I *am* your father," said Zurg.

"No-o-o!" screamed New Buzz.

Rex scrambled down from the top of the elevator and ran up behind Zurg. "Buzz, you could have defeated Zurg all along. You just need to believe in yourself!" said Rex.

Zurg raised his blaster to New Buzz's head. "Prepare to die!" shouted Zurg.

"Ahh, I can't look," said Rex, covering his eyes. As the dinosaur turned away, his tail hit Zurg, knocking him off balance. Zurg teetered on the edge of the elevator and then fell, plunging into the darkness.

"No-o-o!" yelled Zurg.

Rex peered down into the elevator shaft. "I did it! I finally defeated Zurg!"

New Buzz looked down after Zurg. "Father!"

Meanwhile, Buzz and the other toys had managed to slide the elevator's emergency panel open. Inside the elevator, Al stood impatiently with his green suitcase.

While the others held on to his rear end, Slinky lowered himself into the elevator and dangled behind Al. He unlocked Al's case and spotted Woody. As the elevator reached the lobby, Slinky began to pull Woody out of the case. But then the Prospector appeared and pulled Woody back in just as Al stepped out.

Overextended, Slinky sprang back into the elevator—and the other toys came crashing down on top of him. They all ran after Al, but he got into his car and drove off before they could reach him.

"How are we gonna get him now?" asked Rex. Then they spotted an idling Pizza Planet truck.

"Go, go, go!" Buzz shouted, rushing the toys to the truck. He stopped when he noticed New Buzz chasing a ball as it sailed through the air. "Are you coming?" he asked.

New Buzz caught the ball and then threw it

back where it came from. "No," he replied. "I have a lot of catching up to do with my dad."

Buzz looked up to see the ball hit Zurg right in the head. But Zurg wasn't fazed. "Good throw, son. Go long, Buzzy," Zurg called to New Buzz. Then he raised his ion blaster and fired another ball.

"Oh, you're a great dad!" New Buzz shouted as he chased after the ball. "Yippee!"

Buzz gave New Buzz a Space Ranger salute. "Farewell," he said, then raced to join his friends.

Chapter

After the toys climbed into the Pizza Planet truck, Buzz took control of the situation. "Slink, take the pedals. Rex, you navigate." Buzz slid a stack of pizza boxes under the steering wheel and climbed to the top. "Hamm, operate the levers and knobs." Hamm began pushing all the truck's buttons while Rex climbed to the top of the dashboard for a better view.

Suddenly, the toys heard someone say, "Strangers, from the outside!" They looked up to see three green toy aliens hanging from the truck's rearview mirror.

"Oh, no," moaned Buzz.

Then Rex spotted Al. "He's at a red light! We can catch him."

"Maximum power, Slink!" Buzz ordered.

Slinky pushed on the gas pedal with all his might, but the truck wouldn't budge. On the dashboard, Rex peered through the windshield. "It turned green. Hurry!" he called.

"Why won't it go?" asked Buzz.

The aliens pointed to the stick shift. "Use the wand of power," they said.

Hamm helped to get the truck into gear, and suddenly it sped forward.

"Ahh!" yelled Rex as the truck hit a line of orange cones.

"Rex, which way?" asked Buzz.

"Left. I mean right. No, I mean left . . . left is right!" said Rex.

The truck sped down the street, swerving wildly. "Buzz, he's turning left, he's turning left!" cried Rex.

Hamm sat quietly reading the vehicle's owner's manual. "Oh, I seriously doubt he's getting this kind of mileage," he said.

"Go right!" shouted Rex, spotting Al's car.

"Right, right, right!" he repeated frantically.

Buzz cranked the steering wheel, cutting across three lanes of traffic. "Oooooh!" cried the aliens.

Al's car made another turn, sped straight toward the airport, and pulled into the airport's unloading area. The truck followed. The toys parked it on the curb and peered out the window.

"There he is!" said Buzz. He pointed to where Al was checking his case with the ticket agent. Buzz spied a stack of empty pet carriers, and the toys jumped inside one. Hidden inside the pet carrier, they were moved right behind Al.

"The contents of that case are worth more than you make in a year," Al told the ticket agent. "You got that, sport?"

"I understand, sir," the agent replied, placing the case on a conveyor belt.

The toys in the pet carrier were put up on the conveyor belt with all the other bags. "Once we go through, we just need to find that case," said Buzz. The carrier passed through the entrance to the baggage area, which was a gigantic maze of conveyor belts. Hundreds of bags were moving in every direction.

Suddenly, the pet carrier dropped as though on a roller coaster. "Ahhhh!" cried the toys inside. The carrier tumbled onto a lower conveyor belt, bursting open and freeing the toys. "Oww!" they shouted.

"There's the case!" Slinky yelled, pointing to the right.

"No, there's the case!" said Hamm, pointing to the left.

"You take that one, and we'll take this one," said Buzz.

Hamm and Rex unzipped the case on the left, only to find a jumble of camera equipment.

Buzz and Slinky chased after the case on the right. When they reached a fork in the conveyor belt, Slinky's feet got stuck on a bag that was heading in one direction while he and Buzz were going in the other.

"Buzz!" Slinky called. "My back end's going to

Baton Rouge!" He couldn't hold on and snapped in the direction where his feet were stuck—away from Buzz.

Buzz continued to chase after the case. When he spotted it on an upper level, he ran up to it, jumping over luggage on the way.

"Okay, Woody, let's go!" he called as he reached the case. He opened it, only to be punched and knocked off the belt by the Prospector!

The Prospector climbed out and swung his plastic pick at Buzz. "Take that, space toy!"

Suddenly, Woody popped up and grabbed the Prospector. "Hey! No one does that to my friend!" said Woody.

In their struggle, both toys fell out of the case. The Prospector slashed Woody's arm with his pick, and Woody's shoulder started to rip open once again.

"Your choice, Woody!" growled the Prospector. "You can go to Japan together—or in pieces! If he fixed you once, he can fix you again! Now, get in the box."

"Never!" shouted Woody.

"Fine!" The Prospector had raised his pick to land one final blow, when—*Snap! Snap! Snap!*—he was suddenly blinded by bright flashes of light.

Andy's toys were back with the cameras they had found. "Arghhhh!" cried the Prospector.

The momentary distraction gave Buzz enough time to grab the Prospector by the collar and lift him off his feet. "Gotcha!" yelled Buzz triumphantly.

"Idiots!" sputtered the Prospector. "Children destroy toys! You'll all be ruined! Forgotten! Spending eternity rotting in some landfill!"

"I think it's time you learned the true meaning of playtime," said Woody. He pointed down the conveyor belt. "Right over there, guys."

A few minutes later, a little girl retrieved her backpack from the luggage claim and found the Prospector in the front pouch. "Look!" the girl said, placing a doll in the pouch next to him. "A big ugly man doll! Oooh, he needs a makeover."

"Hi!" the doll said to the Prospector when the little girl had strapped the backpack onto her shoulders. "You'll like Amy." The doll turned to look at the Prospector. Half of her face was covered with marker. "She's an artist."

The Prospector shuddered in horror as the little girl carried him out of the baggage claim area.

"Happy trails, Prospector," called Woody as he watched the Prospector go.

"Buzz! Woody!" shouted Slinky.

"Help us out here," called Hamm. They were trying to free Jessie and Bullseye from the case. Bullseye jumped out, but Jessie was still stuck inside. The case was approaching the end of the line and would soon be loaded onto the plane.

"Oh, no—Jessie!" cried Woody.

"Woody!" Jessie yelled as the case went over the edge of the belt. The other toys managed to scramble off the belt just in time. But Jessie plummeted down a steep ramp. The toys watched, terrified, as a baggage handler closed the case, loaded it onto a cart, and drove off.

Woody whistled, and Bullseye galloped forward and slid beneath him.

"C'mon, Buzz!" Woody called, and Buzz jumped on, too.

Bullseye reared up. "Ride like the wind, Bullseye!" yelled Woody. Bullseye jumped off the edge of the belt and took off in pursuit of Jessie.

"Giddyap!" called Woody.

The three toys quickly caught up to the moving luggage cart. "Buzz, give me a boost," said Woody. He climbed onto Buzz's shoulders, getting just high enough to reach and grab on to a luggage tag on the cart.

Suddenly, the cart turned, and Woody was pulled away from Buzz and Bullseye. He gripped the luggage tag desperately. Carefully, he managed to climb up the pile of luggage, finally reaching the top of the cart. He spotted Al's case and ran toward it. But just as he was about to reach it, the cart came to a stop and the baggage handler grabbed the case. Woody watched in horror as the case was loaded onto the plane.

Chapter

Hidden inside a golf bag, Woody was loaded onto the plane, too. Once inside the cargo hold, he unzipped the golf bag, spilling golf balls everywhere. A gigantic pile of luggage surrounded him. He soon spotted Al's case and ran over to open it. Inside, he found a frightened Jessie, curled up in a ball on top of the foam.

"Excuse me, ma'am," said Woody, "but I believe you're on the wrong flight."

"Woody!" said Jessie with relief.

"Come on, Jess. It's time to take you home." Woody helped Jessie out of the case and gave her a hug.

"But what if Andy doesn't like me?" asked Jessie.

"Nonsense," said Woody. "Andy will love you. Besides, he's got a little sister."

"He does?" exclaimed Jessie. "Why didn't you say so? Let's go!"

Woody and Jessie ran behind a suitcase, hiding from the baggage handler. Woody decided to make a move. "Okay, on three. One . . . two—" But before they could escape, the door closed!

"This is bad," said Woody.

"How are we gonna get out of here?" asked Jessie.

"Over there! Come on!" Woody pointed to a stream of light leaking in from the other end of the cargo hold. They ran over and peered through a hatch on the bottom of the plane. They popped open the hatch and looked down at the plane's landing gear below. The plane was already moving quickly down the runway.

"You sure about this?" asked Jessie.

"No! Let's go!" shouted Woody. Together, they climbed down the landing gear toward the plane's wheels. Woody slipped, but luckily

Jessie grabbed his hand in the nick of time.

"Hold on, Woody!" she cried. Under the strain of dangling from Jessie's hand, Woody's arm began to tear. He looked at the ground rushing below him. His hat flew off his head and down the runway . . . before someone grabbed it. It was Buzz!

"What's a cowboy without his hat?" Buzz called as he rode up beside the plane on Bullseye.

"Buzz!" shouted Woody. Then he had an idea. "Buzz, get behind the tires!"

Woody grabbed hold of his pull string. Using it like a lasso, he threw it around a bolt on the plane's landing gear.

"Jessie! Let go of the plane!" he shouted.

"What, are you crazy?" exclaimed Jessie.

"Just pretend it's the final episode of *Woody's Roundup!*" called Woody.

"But it was canceled!" replied Jessie. "We never saw if you made it!"

"Well, then, let's find out together!" said Woody.

Jessie let go of the landing gear, and she and Woody both let out a scream as Woody's pull string swung them both down between the plane's huge wheels. The pull string slipped off the bolt just in time, and Woody and Jessie landed on Bullseye's back, right behind Buzz!

Bullseye slowed to a stop, and the group watched as the plane took off.

"We did it!" yelled Jessie. She leaped off Bullseye and pulled Woody with her, then jumped onto Woody's back.

Buzz climbed down from Bullseye as well. "Nice ropin', cowboy," he said to Woody.

"That was definitely Woody's finest hour!" cried Jessie.

"Your hat, partner," said Buzz as he handed Woody his cowboy hat. Woody twirled it with a laugh.

Suddenly, a plane whooshed over their heads, and the four startled toys looked up in fear. "Let's go home," Woody said.

The Davis van pulled up to the house and stopped. Andy jumped out and ran toward the front door. He burst into his bedroom and began searching his shelf for Woody. But all he could find were some dusty old books.

Disappointed, he turned and looked around the room. On his bed sat Etch, with the words WELCOME HOME, ANDY spelled out on his screen. Surrounding Etch were all of Andy's toys, plus Jessie and Bullseye. Overjoyed, Andy picked up Woody, Jessie, and Bullseye. "Oh, wow! New toys. Thanks, Mom!"

Below Andy's window, the luggage cart from the airport was parked haphazardly in the street.

The next day, Andy repaired Woody's torn arm and gave it a tug. It was as good as new.

"Andy," Mrs. Davis called as she stepped into

Andy's room. "Come on, hon, it's time to go." Then she spotted Woody. "Hey, you fixed Woody!"

"Yeah. I'm glad I decided not to take him to camp," said Andy, setting Woody down on his desk. "His whole arm might have come off."

After Andy had left the room with his mom, Woody sat up and looked at his arm with delight. He realized that Andy hadn't taken him to Cowboy Camp because he had wanted to protect him—not get rid of him.

From across the room came a raucous "Yeehaw!" On Andy's bed, Jessie jumped up and held her boot out to show Bullseye the ANDY that was now scrawled on the sole. "Oh, Bullseye, we're part of a family again!" she exclaimed.

Sitting down, Bullseye lifted his hooves to show Jessie the four letters—A, N, D, and Y— that had been written on each one.

"Ma'am?" Buzz said, approaching Jessie. "I, uh, well, I just want to say you're a bright young woman with a beautiful yarn full of hair . . . hair full of yarn . . . It's a . . . Oh, um . . . I must go."

He started to walk away in embarrassment, but Jessie grabbed him.

"Well, aren't you the sweetest space toy I ever met!" she declared.

Suddenly, they heard the sound of a dog barking. Buster was standing near the door, scratching to get out.

"Bark-bark?" asked Slinky, responding to Buster. Buster continued to whine. "This feller says he needs to go out back for a little private time," Slinky told the toys.

"That critter needs help!" exclaimed Jessie. She ran over to Andy's racetrack and jumped on top of a car, riding it down the ramp like a skateboard. She rounded the loop, bounced on a rubber ball, and went flying toward the doorknob, opening the door to let Buster out. "Yo-de-lay-he-hoo!" she cried.

Buzz just stared at her in awe.

Meanwhile, Hamm was playing the Zurg video game. "Hey, Rex, I could use a hand over here," he said.

"I don't need to play. I've *lived* it," answered Rex with a smug smile.

Hamm pushed frantically on the controller. "No, no, no! Ah, nuts!" he cried as he lost the game.

Suddenly, the screen switched over to a TV channel, and the commercial for Al's Toy Barn appeared.

"Welcome to Al's Toy Barn," said the on-screen Al in a dejected voice. "We've got the lowest prices in town. Everything for a buck, buck, buck." On the last *buck*, he broke down and began to sob.

Hamm and Rex exchanged a look. "Well, I guess crime doesn't pay!" said Hamm.

Nearby, Woody was showing Bo Peep his newly repaired arm. "Andy did a great job, huh? Nice and strong!" He flexed his arm like a body-builder.

"I like it," replied Bo. "It makes you look tough."

Squeak! Squeak! They looked up to see Wheezy hopping over.

"Wheezy! You're fixed!" cried Woody.

"Oh, yeah, Mr. Shark looked in the toy box and found me an extra squeaker," said Wheezy, his voice fully restored.

"And?" asked Woody. "How do you feel?"

"Oh, I feel swell," said Wheezy. "In fact, I think I feel a song coming on!" He grabbed Mike's microphone and began to croon a lively tune. Several toys began dancing.

Woody went over to the windowsill and watched as Andy's sister toddled from Andy to his mom on the driveway below. She was learning to walk.

After a moment, Buzz came over and joined him. "You still worried?" he asked.

"About Andy? Nah," Woody replied. "It'll be fun while it lasts."

"I'm proud of you, cowboy," said Buzz with a smile.

"Besides," said Woody, "when it all ends, I'll have old Buzz Lightyear to keep me company." He gave Buzz a pat on the back. "For infinity . . . and beyond."